This book belongs to

JORDYNN

A Read-Aloud Storybook

Adapted by Jennifer Liberts Weinberg
Illustrated by the Disney Storybook Artists

Random House New York

Printed in the United States of America
September 2002
11

www.randomhouse.com/kids/disney

Cinderella

Every day, Cinderella woke up early to do
chores for her mean Stepmother and stepsisters.
From morning to night, they gave her things to do.
But the birds and mice were Cinderella's friends
and helped her with her work.

One morning, a messenger came from the palace to invite Cinderella and her stepsisters to a royal ball. Cinderella was very excited! But her Stepmother gave her a long list of chores to do before she could go.

While Cinderella was busy working, the birds and mice began fixing an old dress that had belonged to Cinderella's mother. Before long, they'd made Cinderella a beautiful gown!

By the time Cinderella finished her chores,
she thought it was too late to get ready for the ball.
She was very sad.

"Surprise!" The birds and mice gave Cinderella
the finished gown.

"Oh, thank you so much!" she cried.

Cinderella got dressed and rushed to join her stepsisters. But when her stepsisters saw her, they became so jealous they tore Cinderella's lovely gown to pieces!

Cinderella ran to the garden and wept.
Just then, sparkling lights swirled all
around her. It was Cinderella's Fairy
Godmother! "Dry those tears," she said.
"You can't go to the ball looking like that."

13

With a wave of her magic wand, the Fairy Godmother turned a pumpkin into a coach and Cinderella's rags into a gorgeous gown. And with one more wave, Cinderella had tiny glass slippers on her feet.

Before Cinderella left for the ball, she received a warning. "On the stroke of midnight, the spell will be broken," the Fairy Godmother told her. "Everything will be as before."

That night at the ball, the Prince met Cinderella. Without knowing each other's names, they danced and danced until the clock struck midnight.

"I must go!" Cinderella cried. As she fled, she lost a glass slipper on the staircase.

The next day, the Prince announced that he wanted to marry the girl who had lost her glass slipper.

When the wicked Stepmother realized it was Cinderella who was the Prince's favorite, she locked Cinderella in her room!

"Let me out!" Cinderella cried.

The Grand Duke went to every home in the kingdom looking for the maiden whose foot fit the tiny glass shoe.

Cinderella's little friends took the key out of the Stepmother's pocket. They slipped the key under Cinderella's door just in time!

When the Grand Duke put the slipper on Cinderella's foot, it fit perfectly.

Soon after, Cinderella and the Prince were married. And they lived happily ever after!

Snow White

Long ago, there lived a lovely princess named Snow White. Her stepmother, the Queen, was jealous of Snow White's beauty.

Each day, the Queen would ask, "Magic Mirror on the wall, who is the fairest one of all?"

And the Mirror would always answer, "You are."

But one day, the Mirror said, "A lovely maid I see, who is more fair than thee."

The Queen knew it must be Snow White.

Snow White was so beautiful and kind that even a handsome prince who was passing by soon noticed her. Little did he know that when he came into the courtyard to sing to Snow White, the evil Queen was watching nearby.

The Queen was very jealous. Snow White realized she must leave home or risk being hurt by the Queen. Snow White was so frightened that she ran deep into the forest. "Do you know where I can stay?" she asked a group of friendly animals.

The animals led Snow White to a tiny cottage in the woods.

"It's like a doll's house!" said Snow White. She knocked on the door, but no one answered. So she slowly stepped inside.

Snow White found seven tiny bowls, seven tiny chairs, and seven tiny beds. But the cottage was a mess.

"Oh, my! There must be seven tiny children living here! Let's clean the house and surprise them," she said to her animal companions. "Then maybe they'll let me stay."

Soon, seven tiny men
arrived—the Seven Dwarfs!

Snow White promised to wash and
sew and sweep for the little men. In
return, they kept her safe and happy. The
Seven Dwarfs loved having Snow White
stay in their cottage.

Back at the castle, the Magic Mirror told the Queen where Snow White was hiding.

The Queen was so angry that she drank a potion that turned her into an old hag. Then she created a magic apple.

"With one bite of this poisoned apple, Snow White's eyes will close forever," she said. The only cure for the sleeping spell was love's first kiss.

As soon as the Dwarfs went to work, the Queen, disguised as a peddler woman, approached Snow White. The forest animals recognized the Queen and ran off to warn the Dwarfs.

But by the time the Dwarfs arrived, it was too late. Snow White had already taken a bite of the poisoned apple! She fell to the floor in a deep sleep.

The evil Queen fled from the cottage, but the Seven Dwarfs raced after her. They chased the Queen to a rocky cliff. A rock broke beneath her feet and the Queen fell from the mountaintop into the darkness below.

The brokenhearted Dwarfs watched over Snow White day and night. Then one day, the Prince appeared. He had been searching for the beautiful princess.

The Prince kissed Snow White. Moments later, she awakened. The Prince's kiss had broken the spell!

Snow White kissed the Dwarfs on
their foreheads and thanked them for
all they had done. Then the Prince and
Snow White rode off to his castle, where
they lived happily ever after.

Sleeping Beauty

Once upon a time, a kind king and gentle queen had a baby girl named Aurora. Visitors came to see the baby, including King Hubert, who ruled a nearby kingdom, and his young son, Prince Phillip. The two kings decided that Phillip and Aurora would marry one day and unite the kingdoms.

The king and queen were so happy that they held a celebration.

Soon, three good fairies, Flora, Fauna, and Merryweather, arrived. They came to give magical gifts to the baby princess. Flora said, "My gift shall be the gift of beauty." Fauna said, "My gift shall be the gift of song."

But before Merryweather could give her gift, the evil fairy Maleficent appeared! She was so angry she hadn't been invited that she put a curse on the baby. "Before the sun sets on her sixteenth birthday," Maleficent said, "she shall prick her finger on the spindle of a spinning wheel . . . and die."

Merryweather wanted to take away
Maleficent's curse, but her powers were not
strong enough. Instead, she changed the curse.
Aurora wouldn't die, but instead would
fall into a deep sleep. Only true love's kiss
would break the spell.

Then Flora came up with a plan. The three fairies would transform themselves into peasants and raise the princess deep in the forest until her sixteenth birthday. Once the curse ended, they would return Aurora to the palace.

Many years passed, and Maleficent had
lost her patience. It was almost Aurora's
sixteenth birthday, and her evil helpers still
hadn't found the princess. "Sixteen years and
not a trace of her!" Maleficent shouted. "Are
you sure you've searched everywhere?"

51

Meanwhile, Aurora had grown to be sweet and lovely. On her sixteenth birthday, the fairies sent her out to pick berries while they prepared a surprise party. As she wandered about, Aurora sang a song about true love. Nearby, a young prince heard Aurora's pretty voice.

Aurora and the prince met and quickly fell in love. But Aurora wouldn't tell the prince her name because the fairies had warned her never to speak to strangers. Even so, she invited the prince to visit their cottage that night.

Back at the cottage, the fairies were having trouble making Aurora's birthday party extra special. Sure that no one would see them, they decided to use their magic wands. But some magic accidentally escaped up the chimney!

Just as Maleficent's raven was flying overhead, the colorful sparkles from the magic wands shot out of the cottage's chimney. As soon as he saw the magic, the raven flew back to the Forbidden Mountain to tell Maleficent that he had found the good fairies—and the princess!

Aurora returned home and told the fairies all about the handsome stranger she'd met. The fairies explained that she was a princess and was promised to marry Prince Phillip. Then the fairies set off to return the sad princess to her home and to her parents, the king and queen.

When they reached the palace, the fairies left Aurora alone while they went to find her parents. Suddenly a strange glow appeared. In a trance, the princess followed the light to a room with a spinning wheel in it. Maleficent was also in the room.

"Touch the spindle!" the evil fairy commanded. Powerless, the princess obeyed and pricked her finger on the spindle's sharp point. Soon she fell into a deep sleep.

Maleficent then found the prince and locked him in her dungeon.

But shortly after, the good fairies appeared. They realized at last that he was Prince Phillip! They gave him the magical Shield of Virtue and Sword of Truth. "These weapons of righteousness will triumph over evil," they told him.

Maleficent knew Prince Phillip was the only one who could undo her curse on Sleeping Beauty. As he approached the castle, Maleficent turned herself into a terrible dragon and blasted him with red-hot flames. Phillip threw his sword at the dragon with all his might. The beast plunged over the edge of a cliff!

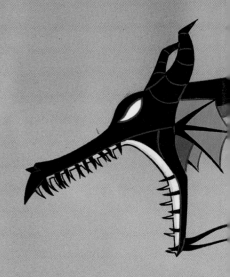

Prince Phillip ran through the palace gates to where Aurora lay. He knelt beside the princess and kissed her gently. Sleeping Beauty awakened and smiled at her prince. Soon after, Princess Aurora married Prince Phillip . . . and they lived happily ever after.